JAN BRETT

Comet's
Nine Lives

PUFFIN BOOKS

For Sean and Yun

PUFFIN BOOKS
Published by the Penguin Group
Penguin Putnam Books for Young Readers,
345 Hudson Street, New York, New York, 10014, U.S.A.
Penguin Books Ltd, 27 Wrights Lane, London W8 5TZ, England
Penguin Books Australia Ltd, Ringwood, Victoria, Australia
Penguin Books Canada Ltd, 10 Alcorn Avenue, Toronto, Ontario,
Canada M4V 3B2
Penguin Books (N.Z.) Ltd, 182-190 Wairau Road, Auckland 10,
New Zealand
Penguin Books Ltd, Registered Offices: Harmondsworth,
Middlesex, England

First Published in the United States of America by G. P. Putnam's
Sons, a division of The Putnam & Grosset Group, 1996
Published by Puffin Books, a division of Penguin Putnam Books
for Young Readers, 2001

10 9 8 7 6

THE LIBRARY OF CONGRESS HAS CATALOGED THE G. P. PUTNAM'S SONS
EDITION AS FOLLOWS:
Brett, Jan, date
Comet's Nine Lives / written and illustrated by Jan Brett. p. cm.
Summary: Comet the cat uses up eight of his nine lives trying to
find the right place to live on Nantucket Island.
[1. Cats—Fiction. 2. Nantucket Island (Mass.)—Fiction. I. Title.
PZ7.B75225Co 1996 [E]—dc20 95-11646 CIP AC
ISBN 0-399-22931-0

This edition ISBN 0-698-11894-4

Manufactured in China.

Comet was born thirty miles out to sea on Nantucket Island. He grew up wandering all over the island, staying a few days here and a few days there.

One summer day Comet stopped in a garden to nibble some tasty looking foxgloves. First they made him feel woozy. Then he fell into a deep sleep.

· One ·

When Comet woke up, he felt fine, but
different. *Oops!* He realized he'd lost the first
of the nine lives every cat has when it is born.

Maybe I should find myself a home.
And he trotted into the bookstore and settled
down on top of a stack of bestsellers.

Life was good until one day it rained all morning and
the islanders hurried inside for something to read.
In the rush, Comet's tower of bestsellers toppled over
and he was buried under a pile of books. *Oh, no!*
He had turned the page on life number two.

I think I need some fresh salt air.
Down to the docks he went and arrived just as a
little scalloper, the *Jean T*, was casting off. Once
under way, an easterly wind blew up and Comet
knew he had made a mistake.

Up, up the *Jean T* rose. Down, down, down she flew
on a following sea. Comet hung on until a huge wave
foamed across the stern and he found himself afloat
on the high seas.

·three·

The tide carried Comet back into the harbor, but
as he flicked the salt from his whiskers, life number
three went out with the tide.

Comet was still recovering on the beach when he heard music. It was the annual Fourth of July concert. He climbed up a tree for a better look.

Four

The music reached its loudest chord. Comet got
so excited that he lost his grip and plunged down
into the tuba. Three waltzes and a Sousa march
later, Comet staggered away, and life number four
sounded its last chord.

Comet spent the night trying to figure out what to do next. He wished there was another cat around to ask if its lives were going by as quickly as his. The next day, everyone was going up to an open window and coming down with ice cream. Comet was hungry so he trotted after the crowd.

The staff at the ice cream shop gave Comet his own bowl of leftover milkshake. He felt so welcome that he decided to stay. But all too soon an island health officer burst into the shop and spotted Comet. "Furball!" he cried. "Feline residues! Maximum infractions!"

Startled, Comet jumped up and fell headfirst into a
strawberry shake. The staff pulled him out and he
watched life number five fly off licking its paws.

Maybe I'm trying too hard. It's time for some fun!
He climbed into a bike basket just as a crowd of
summer visitors were hurrying off the ferry.

It was Waffles' first time on the island.
She was happy to have Comet's company,
and off they went bumpity, bump all around
the island. Just as they reached the bottom
of the last hill into the village, Waffles
screeched to a halt to avoid a taxi.

Comet went flying, along with life number six.
I think I'll just walk the rest of the way.

Six

Comet was limping by the island theater when a poster
advertising the last performance of summer caught his eye.
A beautiful actress with a sweet smile looked out at him.
Maybe she would like to take a cat home with her.

Comet pranced happily on stage and purred loudly. The actress sneezed. "There's a cat in here!" she shrieked. "I'm allergic to cats!" She spotted Comet and hurled her sequined high heel right at him.

Comet flew through the air into the last row. The
curtain had come down on life number seven!

Fall breezes were blowing up as the summer visitors
headed for the ferry. Comet wandered alone along the
beach. He could see the red beacon of the Brant Point
lighthouse in the distance.

Waves crashed and pounded on the sand. The wind
picked up and deck chairs and lobster pots flew by
Comet. It was Hurricane Elmadore heading straight
for Nantucket Island. All Comet could see now was
the blinking lighthouse beacon. He ran toward it
when a huge wave broke on top of him.

The rushing surf carried Comet into an open doorway, as life number eight washed out to sea. Dazed, he opened his eyes and saw a green light across the room.
"Meow," someone purred.
"Meow," he answered, looking up.
He was staring into the green eyes of the lighthouse cat.
At that moment, he knew he was home.

And as the fall days turned into winter, Comet knew exactly where he wanted to live for the rest of his life.